Usborne
Christmas Tunes

Anthony Marks

Designed and illustrated by
Candice Whatmore

Edited by Kirsteen Rogers

Music selected, arranged and edited by
Anthony Marks and Catherine Duffy
New compositions by Anthony Marks
Music setting: Andrew Jones

About this book

This book contains a collection of Christmas carols, songs and other music associated with winter. The carols have been arranged for voice and piano. Additionally, the top line can be played by a melody instrument such as recorder or violin. (Where there is more than one note in the top line, the melody always follows the upper note.) The rest of the tunes have been arranged as pieces to be played on the piano. Each song has a short piano introduction. You can use this at the start of each verse, or you can play the introduction just once at the beginning of the song and start later verses after the double barline.

At the top of each carol is a metronome mark which tells you what speed to sing and play. But these marks are only suggestions – you may prefer a different speed.

As an alternative, use the guitar chords above the stave to accompany the melody line. The diagrams below show you how to play all the chords you need for this book.

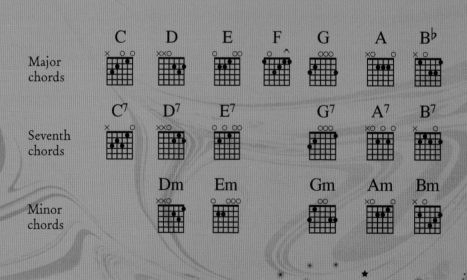

Internet links

If you have a computer, you can listen to all the pieces in this book on the Usborne Quicklinks Website to hear how they go, or to sing or play along to. Just go to www.usborne-quicklinks.com and type in the keywords "christmas tunes", then follow the simple instructions.

Contents

Every effort has been made to trace the copyright holders of the material in this book. If any rights have been omitted, the publishers offer their sincere apologies and will rectify this in any subsequent editions following notification. The publishers are grateful to DesignEXchange Company Limited for their permission to reproduce marbling effects (© 2003).

First published in 2008 by Usborne Publishing Ltd, Usborne House, 83–85 Saffron Hill, London ECIN 8RT, England. www.usborne.com Copyright © 2008 Usborne Publishing Ltd. The name Usborne and the devices ♀⛵ are Trade Marks of Usborne Publishing Ltd. All rights reserved. No part of this publication may be reproduced, stored in a retrieval system, or transmitted in any form or by any means, electronic, mechanical, photocopying, recording or otherwise, without the prior permission of the publisher. UE. First published in America 2008. Printed in China

The first Nowell

"Nowell" is an old English word for Christmas or Christmas carol. It comes from the French word "Noël", so some people think this song is French. But it was probably first sung in Cornwall, in southwest England, in the 16th century.

The first Nowell the angel did say
Was to certain poor shepherds in fields as they lay.
In fields where they lay keeping their sheep,
On a cold winter's night that was so deep.
Nowell, Nowell, Nowell, Nowell,
Born is the King of Israel!

They looked up and saw a star
Shining in the East, beyond them far;
And to the earth it gave great light,
And so it continued both day and night.
Nowell, Nowell . . .

And by the light of that same star
Three wise men came from country far;
To seek for a king was their intent,
And to follow the star wherever it went.
Nowell, Nowell . . .

This star drew nigh to the northwest;
O'er Bethlehem it took its rest,
And there it did both stop and stay
Right over the place where Jesus lay.
Nowell, Nowell . . .

Then entered in those wise men three,
Full reverently upon their knee,
And offered there in his presence
Their gold and myrrh and frankincense.
Nowell, Nowell . . .

Then let us all with one accord
Sing praises to our heavenly Lord,
That has made heav'n and earth of nought,
And with his blood mankind has bought.
Nowell, Nowell . . .

Good King Wenceslas

Robustly ♩ = 112

Good King Wen - ces - las looked out,

On the Feast of Ste - phen, When the snow lay round a - bout, Deep and crisp and

e - ven. Bright-ly shone the moon that night, Though the frost was cru - el,

When a poor man came in sight, Gath'-ring win - ter fu - el.

King Wenceslas was Duke of Bohemia (now part of the Czech Republic) in the early 10th century. He was later adopted as the Czech Republic's patron saint. The carol is traditionally sung at Christmas because its story takes place on St. Stephen's feast day – December 26th.

1 Good King Wenceslas looked out,
On the Feast of Stephen,
When the snow lay round about,
Deep and crisp and even.
Brightly shone the moon that night,
Though the frost was cruel,
When a poor man came in sight,
Gath'ring winter fuel.

2 "Hither, page, and stand by me,
If you know it, telling,
Yonder peasant, who is he?
Where and what his dwelling?"
"Sire, he lives a good league hence,
Underneath the mountain,
Right against the forest fence,
By Saint Agnes' fountain."

3 "Bring me flesh and bring me wine,
Bring me pine logs hither:
You and I will see him dine,
When we bear them thither."
Page and monarch, forth they went,
Forth they went together;
Through the rude wind's wild lament,
And the bitter weather.

4 "Sire, the night is darker now,
And the wind blows stronger;
Fails my heart, I know not how;
I can go no longer."
"Mark my footsteps, my good page,
Tread you in them boldly:
You will find the winter's rage
Freeze your blood less coldly."

5 In his master's steps he trod,
Where the snow lay dinted;
Heat was in the very sod
Which the Saint had printed.
Therefore, Christian men, be sure,
Wealth or rank possessing,
Those of you who bless the poor,
Shall yourselves find blessing.

7

Silent night

Franz Gruber was an Austrian teacher and organist. On
December 24 in 1818, a priest named Josef Mohr showed him a
Christmas poem he had written. Gruber quickly composed the
melody and the two men sang the song – called "Stille Nacht"
in German – at their church's Christmas Eve service.

Silent night, holy night,
All is calm, all is bright.
Round yon virgin mother and child,
Holy infant so tender and mild.
Sleep in heavenly peace,
Sleep in heavenly peace.

Silent night, holy night,
Shepherds quake at the sight.
Glory streams from heaven afar,
Heav'nly hosts sing Alleluia.
Christ the Saviour is born,
Christ the Saviour is born.

Silent night, holy night,
Son of God, love's pure light.
Radiance beams from thy holy face,
With the dawn of redeeming grace,
Jesus, Lord, at thy birth,
Jesus, Lord, at thy birth.

Il est né le divin enfant

Because the tune sounds like horn music, this 18th-century French carol may be based on a hunting song that was popular at the time. Try to make the left-hand chords sound like bagpipes. When you get to the end, play from the beginning again, and finish when you get to the "Fine" mark.

Gaudete

"Gaudete" means "rejoice" in Latin. The first part of
this tune was originally published in 1582, in a collection
of carols and sacred songs called "Piae Cantiones". Its
second part is even older. The simple chords in the left
hand are typical of music from the Middle Ages.

O come, all ye faithful

Although the music was written in the 18th century, the original words, which were in Latin, are probably about 500 years older. The verse that begins "Yea, Lord, we greet thee, born this happy morning" is usually only sung on Christmas Day.

1 O come, all ye faithful,
Joyful and triumphant,
O come ye, o come ye to Bethlehem!
Come and behold him
Born the King of Angels:

O come, let us adore him,
O come, let us adore him,
O come, let us adore him,
Christ the Lord!

2 God of God,
Light of Light,
Lo! he abhors not the Virgin's womb;
Very God,
Begotten, not created:

O come, let us adore him . . .

3 Sing, choirs of angels,
Sing in exultation,
Sing, all ye citizens of heaven above;
Glory to God
In the highest:

O come, let us adore him . . .

4 Yea, Lord, we greet thee,
Born this happy morning,
Jesu, to thee be glory giv'n;
Word of the Father,
Now in flesh appearing:

O come, let us adore him . . .

Deck the hall

The tune is thought to have been borrowed from a 16th-century Welsh New Year song. In verse 2, "Yule" is short for Yule log. Yule was an ancient midwinter festival when special logs were burned. This later became a Christmas tradition too.

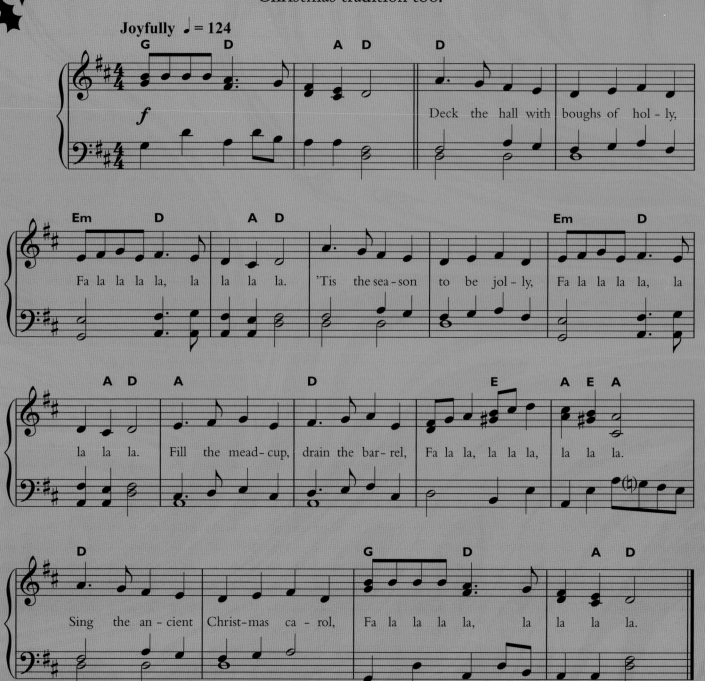

Deck the hall with boughs of hol-ly,

Fa la la la la, la la la la. 'Tis the sea-son to be jol-ly, Fa la la la la, la

la la la. Fill the mead-cup, drain the bar-rel, Fa la la, la la la, la la la.

Sing the an-cient Christ-mas ca-rol, Fa la la la la, la la la la.

Deck the hall with boughs of holly,
Fa la la la la, la la la la.
'Tis the season to be jolly,
Fa la la la la, la la la la.
Fill the mead-cup, drain the barrel,
Fa la la, la la la, la la la.
Sing the ancient Christmas carol,
Fa la la la la, la la la la.

See the blazing Yule before us,
Fa la la la la, la la la la.
Strike the harp and join the chorus,
Fa la la la la, la la la la.
Follow me in merry measure,
Fa la la, la la la, la la la.
While I tell of Yuletide treasure,
Fa la la la la, la la la la.

Fast away the old year passes,
Fa la la la la, la la la la.
Hail the new, ye lads and lasses,
Fa la la la la, la la la la.
Sing we joyous, all together,
Fa la la, la la la, la la la.
Heedless of the wind and weather,
Fa la la la la, la la la la.

God rest ye merry, gentlemen

In the 19th century, town watchmen sang this song as they walked through the streets at Christmastime, hoping to earn extra money at rich people's houses. "God rest ye merry," means "May God keep you strong."

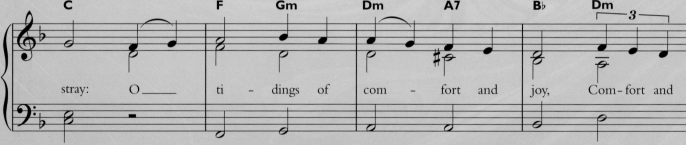

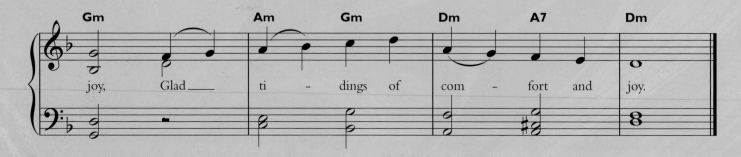

1 God rest ye merry, gentlemen,
Let nothing you dismay,
For Jesus Christ our Saviour
Was born on Christmas Day!
To save us all from Satan's pow'r
When we had gone astray:

O tidings of comfort and joy,
Comfort and joy,
Glad tidings of comfort and joy.

2 In Bethlehem in Jewry
This blessèd babe was born,
And laid within a manger
Upon this blessèd morn,
Which his good mother Mary
Did nothing take in scorn:

O tidings of comfort and joy . . .

3 From God, our heav'nly Father,
A blessèd angel came,
And unto certain shepherds
Brought tidings of the same,
That there was born in Bethlehem
The Son of God by name:

O tidings of comfort and joy . . .

4 But when they came to Bethlehem
Where our dear Saviour lay,
They found him in a manger,
Where oxen feed on hay;
His mother Mary kneeling,
Unto the Lord did pray:

O tidings of comfort and joy . . .

5 Now to the Lord sing praises,
All you within this place
And with true love and brotherhood
Each other now embrace;
This holy tide of Christmas
All others does deface:

O tidings of comfort and joy . . .

How far is it to Bethlehem?

No one knows who wrote this tune, but it is hundreds of
years old. The carol is about a journey to Bethlehem, to
visit the baby Jesus. Play it softly, like a lullaby.

Slowly and gently ♩ = 96

Coventry carol

Slowly and sadly ♩ = 88

mp

Lul – ly lul – la, thou lit – tle ti – ny child, By by, lul – ly lul – lay. O sis – ters too, what may we do, For to pre – serve this day *mf* This poor young thing, For whom we do sing? *mp* By by, lul – ly lul – lay.

This old English carol was part of a nativity play called
"The Pageant of the Shearmen and Tailors", which was first
performed in the 16th century in the city of Coventry. It
is about King Herod's order to kill all the baby boys in
Bethlehem, and the sorrow their mothers felt.

Hark! the herald angels sing

The words of this English carol were written in the 18th century by Charles Wesley, a preacher, who wanted them sung slowly to a solemn tune. Years later, the words were combined with this melody, which is by the German composer Felix Mendelssohn.

Not too quickly ♩ = 96

Hark! the her - ald an - gels sing,—

"Glo - ry to the new - born King." Peace on earth, and mer - cy mild,— God and sin - ners

re - con - ciled. Joy - ful, all you na - tions rise,— Join the tri - umph of the skies.—

With an - gel - ic hosts pro - claim, "Christ is— born in Beth - le - hem."

Hark! the her - ald an - gels sing, "Glo - ry— to the new - born King."

Hark! the herald angels sing,
"Glory to the new-born King."
Peace on earth, and mercy mild,
God and sinners reconciled.
Joyful, all you nations rise,
Join the triumph of the skies.
With angelic hosts proclaim,
"Christ is born in Bethlehem."

Hark! the herald angels sing,
"Glory to the new-born King."

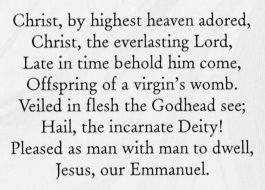

Christ, by highest heaven adored,
Christ, the everlasting Lord,
Late in time behold him come,
Offspring of a virgin's womb.
Veiled in flesh the Godhead see;
Hail, the incarnate Deity!
Pleased as man with man to dwell,
Jesus, our Emmanuel.

Hark! the herald angels sing,
"Glory to the new-born King."

Hail, the heaven-born Prince of Peace!
Hail, the Sun of Righteousness!
Light and life to all he brings,
Risen with healing in his wings.
Mild he lays his glory by,
Born that man no more may die,
Born to raise the sons of earth,
Born to give them second birth.

Hark! the herald angels sing,
"Glory to the new-born King."

Jingle bells

"Jingle bells" was originally a Thanksgiving song,
written by an American minister for his Sunday School.
It was so popular that people began to sing it at
Christmas as well, and it is now more associated
with that time of year.

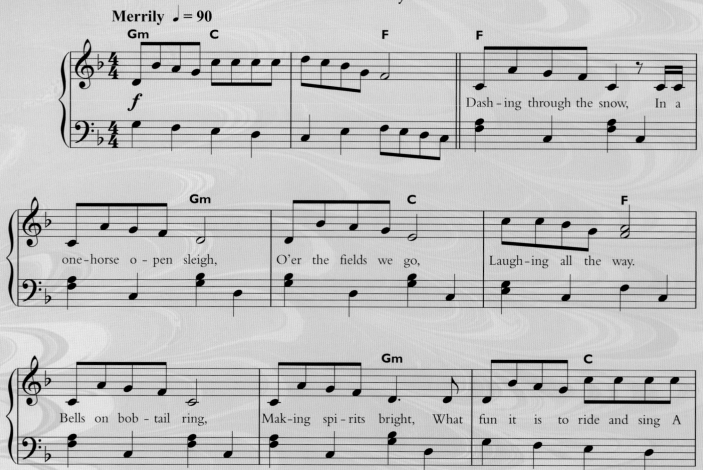

Dashing through the snow,
In a one-horse open sleigh,
O'er the fields we go,
Laughing all the way.
Bells on bob-tail ring,
Making spirits bright,
What fun it is to ride and sing
A sleighing song tonight!

Oh, jingle bells, jingle bells,
Jingle all the way.
Oh what fun it is to ride
In a one-horse open sleigh!
Oh, jingle bells, jingle bells,
Jingle all the way.
Oh what fun it is to ride
In a one-horse open sleigh!

A day or two ago,
I thought I'd take a ride
And soon Miss Fannie Bright
Was seated by my side.
The horse was lean and lank,
Misfortune seem'd his lot,
He got into a drifted bank
And then we got upsot!

Oh, jingle bells, jingle bells,
Jingle all the way.
Oh what fun it is to ride
In a one-horse open sleigh!
Oh, jingle bells, jingle bells,
Jingle all the way.
Oh what fun it is to ride
In a one-horse open sleigh!

Still, still, still

The tune of this traditional Austrian carol is known as the
"Salzburg melody". Nobody knows who wrote the music
or the words, which are in German. "Still, still, still" is a
lullaby for the baby Jesus, so play it very softly and gently.

Rocking carol

This old Czech tune was traditionally sung on
Christmas Eve by children in the Czech Republic.
They believed that while they were singing, Jesus would
arrive secretly, bringing their Christmas presents.

The holly and the ivy

The tradition of decorating houses with holly and ivy comes from ancient winter festivals, when people hoped that they, like the evergreen leaves, would be able to survive the harsh weather. The words for this old English carol come from Somerset or Gloucester. They weave together Christian ideas with much older ones.

The holly and the ivy,
When they are both full grown,
Of all the trees that are in the wood,
The holly bears the crown.

The rising of the sun,
And the running of the deer,
The playing of the merry organ,
Sweet singing in the choir.

The holly bears a blossom,
As white as any flower,
And Mary bore sweet Jesus Christ,
To be our sweet saviour.

The rising of the sun . . .

The holly bears a berry,
As red as any blood,
And Mary bore sweet Jesus Christ
To do poor sinners good.

The rising of the sun . . .

The holly bears a prickle,
As sharp as any thorn,
And Mary bore sweet Jesus Christ
On Christmas Day in the morn.

The rising of the sun . . .

The holly bears a bark
As bitter as any gall,
And Mary bore sweet Jesus Christ
For to redeem us all.

The rising of the sun . . .

It came upon the midnight clear

Smoothly, not too fast ♩ = 88

f

It__ came u - pon the__ mid - night clear, That glo - rious song__ of old, From__ an - gels bend - ing near the earth To__ touch__ their harps of gold: *mp* "Peace on the earth, good - will to men, From heaven's all gra - cious King!" *f* The world in sol - emn__ still - ness lay To__ hear__ the an - gels sing.

There are two tunes to this 19th-century carol.
This one is a traditional English melody, which was
adapted by a composer named Arthur Sullivan. The
words were written by an American pastor.

It came upon the midnight clear,
That glorious song of old,
From angels bending near the earth
To touch their harps of gold:
"Peace on the earth, goodwill to men,
From heaven's all gracious King!"
The world in solemn stillness lay
To hear the angels sing.

Still through the cloven skies they come,
With peaceful wings unfurled;
And still their heav'nly music floats
O'er all the weary world:
Above its sad and lowly plains
They bend on hov'ring wing,
And ever o'er its Babel sounds
The blessèd angels sing.

O ye beneath life's crushing load,
Whose forms are bending low,
Who toil along the climbing way
With painful steps and slow;
Look now, for glad and golden hours
Come swiftly on the wing;
Oh rest beside the weary road
And hear the angels sing.

For lo! the days are hastening on,
By prophets seen of old,
When with the ever-circling years
Shall come the time foretold,
When the new heav'n and earth shall own
The Prince of Peace, their King,
And the whole world send back the song
Which now the angels sing.

Here we come a-wassailing

Wassailing was an old English custom of singing carols door to door. The singers carried a bowl of wassail, a warm, spicy drink. After singing, they shared the wassail with the householders and were given food and drink. Everyone then exchanged good wishes.

Quickly and boldly ♩.= 108

f

Here we come a - was - sail-ing A - mong the leaves so

green, Here we come a - wan-der-ing So fair___ to be seen. Love and joy come to

you, And to you your was - sail too, And God bless you, and send___ you a

hap - py New Year, And God send you a hap - py New Year.

1 Here we come a-wassailing
Among the leaves so green,
Here we come a-wandering
So fair to be seen.

Love and joy come to you,
And to you your wassail too,
And God bless you, and send
you a happy New Year,
And God send you a happy New Year.

2 Our wassail cup is made
Of the rosemary tree,
And so is your beer
Of the best barley.

Love and joy come to you . . .

3 We are not daily beggars
That beg from door to door,
But we are neighbours' children
Whom you have seen before.

Love and joy come to you . . .

4 Good master and good mistress,
As you sit by the fire,
Pray think of us poor children
Who wander in the mire.

Love and joy come to you . . .

5 We have a little purse
Made of leather skin;
We want some of your small change
To line it well within.

Love and joy come to you . . .

6 Call up the butler of this house,
Put on his golden ring;
Let him bring us a glass of beer,
And better we shall sing.

Love and joy come to you . . .

7 Bring us out a table,
And spread it with a cloth;
Bring us out a mouldy cheese,
And some of your Christmas loaf.

Love and joy come to you . . .

8 God bless the master of this house,
Likewise the mistress too;
And all the little children
That round the table go.

Love and joy come to you . . .

Les trois rois

Very rhythmic ♩ = 108

"Les trois rois" ("The three kings") is a very old Christmas
song from Provence in the south of France. In the 19th
century, a French composer named Georges Bizet used it
in some music for a play called "L'Arlésienne", which was
about a woman from Arles, a town in Provence.

Patapan

This French carol tells of the birth of Jesus from the point of view of the shepherds, with their pipes and drums. The word "Patapan" imitates a drum's sound. The drum rhythms are in the left hand, the piper's tune in the right.

Away in a manger

A manger is a long trough that contains hay or straw for feeding animals, and lowing is another word for mooing. Sing and play this carol quietly and gently, like a lullaby.

Gently ♩ = 88

A - way in a mang - ger, no crib for a bed, The lit - tle Lord Je - sus lay down his sweet head. The stars in the bright sky looked down where he lay, The lit - tle Lord Je - sus a - sleep on the hay.

Away in a manger, no crib for a bed,
The little Lord Jesus lay down his sweet head.
The stars in the bright sky looked down where he lay,
The little Lord Jesus asleep on the hay.

The cattle are lowing, the baby awakes,
But little Lord Jesus no crying he makes.
I love thee, Lord Jesus! Look down from the sky,
And stay by my side until morning is nigh.

Be near me, Lord Jesus; I ask thee to stay
Close by me for ever, and love me, I pray.
Bless all the dear children in thy tender care,
And fit us for heaven, to live with thee there.

Ding dong! merrily on high

Church bells were traditionally rung to call people to
church and the "matin chime" was rung before the
morning service. "Gloria, hosanna in excelsis" is
Latin for "Glory, praise in heaven".

Ding dong! merrily on high, in heav'n the bells are ringing.
Ding dong! verily the sky is riv'n with angels singing.

Gloria, Hosanna in excelsis!
Gloria, Hosanna in excelsis!

And on earth below, below, let steeple bells be swungen,
And i-o, i-o, i-o, by priest and people sungen.

Gloria, Hosanna in excelsis!
Gloria, Hosanna in excelsis!

Pray you dutifully prime your matin chime, you ringers,
May you beautifully rhyme your eve-time song, you singers.

Gloria, Hosanna in excelsis!
Gloria, Hosanna in excelsis!

O little town of Bethlehem

The words to this American carol were written in the 19th
century by Phillips Brooks, a rector from Philadelphia. It has
two well-known tunes. This one, by an organist named
Lewis Redner, is more popular in the USA.

O little town of Bethlehem,
How still we see thee lie!
Above thy deep and dreamless sleep
The silent stars go by.
Yet in thy dark streets shineth
The everlasting light.
The hopes and fears of all the years
Are met in thee tonight.

O morning stars, together
Proclaim the holy birth.
And praises sing to God the King,
And peace to men on earth.
For Christ is born of Mary;
And, gathered all above,
While mortals sleep, the angels keep
Their watch of wond'ring love.

How silently, how silently
The wondrous gift is giv'n.
So God imparts to human hearts
The blessings of his heav'n.
No ear may hear his coming,
But in this world of sin,
Where meek souls will receive him, still
The dear Christ enters in.

O holy child of Bethlehem,
Descend to us we pray.
Cast out our sin, and enter in,
Be born in us today.
We hear the Christmas angels
The great glad tidings tell:
O come to us, abide with us,
Our Lord Emmanuel.

Winter

Vivaldi, an Italian composer, wrote a set of violin concertos
called "The four seasons" in 1723. They were inspired by
four poems, which describe the four seasons of the year.
This music reflects the comfort of sitting by the fire,
while people outside are soaked by icy rain.

I saw three ships

There are various ideas about the meaning of this 15th-century English carol. Some people think the three ships represent the three wise men; others say they stand for Mary, Joseph and Jesus.

1 I saw three ships come sailing in,
  On Christmas Day, on Christmas Day,
  I saw three ships come sailing in,
  On Christmas Day in the morning.

2 And what was in those ships all three?
  On Christmas Day, on Christmas Day,
  And what was in those ships all three?
  On Christmas Day in the morning.

3 Our Saviour Christ and his lady,
  On Christmas Day, on Christmas Day,
  Our Saviour Christ and his lady,
  On Christmas Day in the morning.

4 Pray, whither sailed those ships all three?
  On Christmas Day, on Christmas Day,
  Pray, whither sailed those ships all three?
  On Christmas Day in the morning.

5 O they sailed into Bethlehem,
  On Christmas Day, on Christmas Day,
  O they sailed into Bethlehem,
  On Christmas Day in the morning.

6 And all the bells on earth shall ring,
  On Christmas Day, on Christmas Day,
  And all the bells on earth shall ring,
  On Christmas Day in the morning.

7 And all the angels in heav'n shall sing,
  On Christmas Day, on Christmas Day,
  And all the angels in heav'n shall sing,
  On Christmas Day in the morning.

8 And all the souls on earth shall sing,
  On Christmas Day, on Christmas Day,
  And all the souls on earth shall sing,
  On Christmas Day in the morning.

9 Then let us all rejoice amain!
  On Christmas Day, on Christmas Day,
  Then let us all rejoice amain!
  On Christmas Day in the morning.

See amid the winter's snow

An English vicar's son named Edward Caswall wrote
the words for this carol, which was first published
under the title "Hymn for Christmas Day" in 1871.
The music was composed by John Goss, who was
an organist at London's St. Paul's Cathedral.

1 See amid the winter's snow,
Born for us on earth below;
See the tender Lamb appears,
Promis'd from eternal years.

Hail, thou ever-blessèd morn!
Hail, redemption's happy dawn!
Sing through all Jerusalem,
Christ is born in Bethlehem.

2 Lo, within a manger lies
He who built the starry skies;
He who, throned in height sublime,
Sits amid the cherubim.

Hail, thou ever-blessèd morn! . .

3 Say, ye holy shepherds, say
What your joyful news today;
Wherefore have ye left your sheep
On the lonely mountain steep?

Hail, thou ever-blessèd morn! . .

4 "As we watched at dead of night,
Lo, we saw a wondrous light;
Angels singing, "Peace on earth"
Told us of the Saviour's birth."

Hail, thou ever-blessèd morn! . .

5 Sacred infant, all divine,
What a tender love was thine,
Thus to come from highest bliss
Down to such a world as this.

Hail, thou ever-blessèd morn! . .

6 Teach, O teach us, Holy Child,
By thy face so meek and mild,
Teach us to resemble thee,
In thy sweet humility!

Hail, thou ever-blessèd morn! . .

Snow song

Both pieces of music on these pages were written
especially for this book. When you play this piece,
it might help to imagine delicate snowflakes as they
twirl and swirl softly to the ground.

Santa in the snow

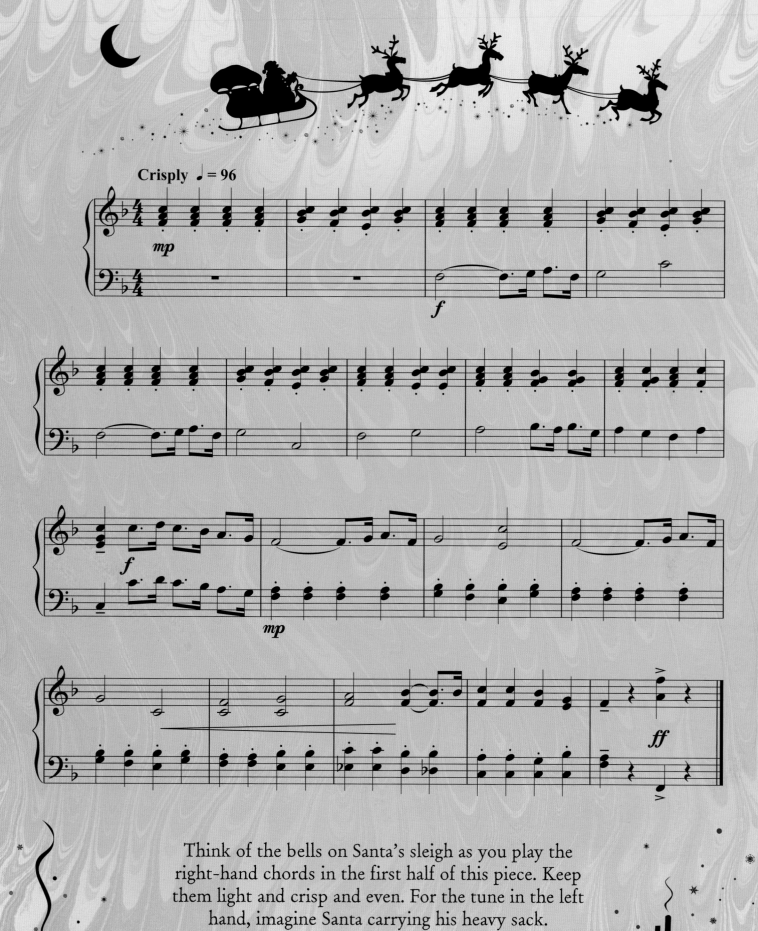

Think of the bells on Santa's sleigh as you play the right-hand chords in the first half of this piece. Keep them light and crisp and even. For the tune in the left hand, imagine Santa carrying his heavy sack.

Go, tell it on the mountain

"Go, tell it on the mountain" is an African-American
spiritual – a song first sung by slaves in the southern USA.
It was first published in Nashville, Tennessee, in 1907 by
John Wesley Work, a composer and collector of folk tunes.

Go, tell it on the mountain,
Over the hills and everywhere,
Go, tell it on the mountain
That Jesus Christ is born!

While shepherds kept their watching
O'er silent flocks by night,
Behold, throughout the heavens
There shone a holy light.

Go, tell it on the mountain . . .

The shepherds feared and trembled,
When lo! above the earth,
Rang out the angels' chorus
That hailed the Saviour's birth.

si - lent flocks by night, Be - hold, through - out the hea - vens There shone a ho - ly light. *cresc.* Go, tell it on the moun - tain, O - ver the hills and e - very - where,___ Go, tell it on the moun - tain That Je - sus Christ is born!

Go, tell it on the mountain . . .

Down in a lowly manger
The humble Christ was born,
And God sent us salvation
That blessèd Christmas morn.

O holy night

On Christmas Eve 1906, a Canadian inventor named
Reginald Fessenden made what many people think was
the first radio broadcast. The broadcast included him
playing "O holy night" on the violin, which makes
this tune the first to be broadcast live on the radio.

Slow down gradually

We three kings of orient are

John Henry Hopkins, an American clergyman, wrote
this carol in 1857. It is really a carol for Epiphany (a feast
celebrated on January 6 to remember the three kings' visit to
Jesus), but it is popular throughout the Christmas season.

1 We three kings of orient are,
Bearing gifts we travel afar,
Field and fountain, moor and mountain,
Following yonder star.

O star of wonder, star of might,
Star with royal beauty bright!
Westward leading, still proceeding,
Guide us to thy perfect light.

2 Born a king on Bethlehem's plain,
Gold I bring, to crown him again,
King forever, ceasing never,
Over us all to reign.

O star of wonder, star of might . . .

3 Frankincense to offer have I,
Incense owns a deity nigh.
Prayer and praising, all men raising,
Worshipping God most high.

O star of wonder, star of might . . .

4 Myrrh is mine, its bitter perfume
Breathes a life of gathering gloom;
Sorrowing, sighing, bleeding, dying,
Sealed in the stone-cold tomb.

O star of wonder, star of might . . .

5 Glorious now behold him arise,
King and God and sacrifice,
Alleluia, alleluia,
Earth to the heav'ns replies.

O star of wonder, star of might . . .

Skaters' waltz

A waltz is a graceful, lilting dance. This tune
was written as a piece for orchestra in 1822 by a
French composer named Emile Waldteufel. He
was inspired by watching people ice skating at a
rink in the Bois de Boulogne, a park in Paris.

While shepherds watched their flocks

Solemnly ♩ = 100

While shep - herds watched their
flocks by night, All seat - ed on the ground, The an - gel of the
Lord came down, And glo - ry shone a - round.

The writers of this English carol, Nahum Tate and Nicholas Brady, were the first to rewrite Bible verses in rhyme for people to sing in church. They wrote the words of "While shepherds watched" in 1703; the tune is by an English composer, George Frederick Handel.

While shepherds watched their flocks by night,
All seated on the ground,
The angel of the Lord came down,
And glory shone around.

"Fear not," said he, for mighty dread
Had seized their troubled mind,
"Glad tidings of great joy I bring
To you and all mankind.

"To you in David's town this day
Is born of David's line
A Saviour, who is Christ the Lord,
And this shall be the sign:

"The heav'nly babe you there shall find
To human view displayed,
All meanly wrapped in swathing bands,
And in a manger laid."

Thus spake the seraph, and forthwith
Appeared a shining throng
Of angels praising God, who thus
Addressed their joyful song:

"All glory be to God on high,
And to the earth be peace,
Goodwill henceforth from heaven to men;
Begin and never cease."

Bring a torch, Jeanette, Isabella

This old French carol tells an imaginary tale of two milkmaids who
go to milk their cows, and find the baby Jesus asleep in the hay.
They rush back to their village to share the news and everyone
comes to see the baby, carrying flaming torches to light their way.

Bring a torch, Jeanette, Isabella,
Bring a torch, come swiftly and run!
Christ is born, tell the folk of the village,
Jesus is sleeping in his cradle.
Ah! ah! Beautiful is the mother,
Ah! ah! Beautiful is her son!

It is wrong when the Child is sleeping
It is wrong to talk so loud;
Silence, all, as you gather around,
Lest your noise should waken Jesus.
Hush! hush! See how fast he slumbers!
Hush! hush! See how fast he sleeps!

Hasten now, good folk of the village;
Hasten now the Christ Child to see.
You will find him asleep in the manger;
Quietly come and whisper softly.
Hush! hush! Peacefully now he slumbers.
Hush! hush! Peacefully now he sleeps.

We wish you a merry Christmas

Like "Here we come a-wassailing" on page 30, this 16th-century carol describes the custom of carol-singing in wealthy houses in return for refreshments. The carol is thought to come from southwest England, but no one is sure who wrote it.

We wish you a merry Christmas,
We wish you a merry Christmas,
We wish you a merry Christmas,
And a happy New Year!

Good tidings we bring,
To you and your kin;
We wish you a merry Christmas,
And a happy New Year!

We all want some figgy pudding,
We all want some figgy pudding,
We all want some figgy pudding,
So bring some out here!

Good tidings we bring . . .

We won't go until we've got some,
We won't go until we've got some,
We won't go until we've got some,
So bring some out here!

Good tidings we bring . . .

The shepherds' farewell

Hector Berlioz, the 19th-century French composer who wrote this carol, scribbled down the music at a party, because he was bored. He later added words about the shepherds saying goodbye to Mary, Joseph and Jesus, who were fleeing for Egypt.

Smoothly ♩. = 38

O Christmas tree

There are many versions and translations of this German carol.
Its oldest words are thought to have been written around 1550.
The tune is a traditional folk melody, which has also been
adopted for the state songs of four states of the USA.

Dance of the Sugar Plum Fairy

This music is from "The Nutcracker", a ballet written by a Russian composer named Tchaikovsky. In the story, a girl dreams that her soldier-shaped nutcracker turns into a prince. He takes her to a magical land where she meets the Sugar Plum Fairy.

Mysteriously ♩ = 120